A LETTER TO PARENTS AND ALL LOVERS OF CHILDREN
From Drs. Robin and Stephen Larsen

A childhood filled with unconditional love, a safe yet varied environment, and lots of inter-action with others will create the optimal conditions for raising a healthy, curious, intelligent child. But there is another dimension to consider. Joseph Campbell has shown us how, knowingly or unknowingly, we **live our myths**. They are the **soul stories** we tell with our lives.

By introducing your child to Gina Otto's truly wise, as well as beautiful book, you will reaffirm your child's sense of selfhood. Cassandra doesn't find affirmation in her critical, controlling, and self-important world, so she embarks on a vision quest to find her rock — her still place within. It is there that her personal convictions emerge, allowing her to receive inspiration from her higher self — a wise and beautiful Angel.

This book shows children how to extract wisdom from adversity by looking within for their empowerment — Joseph Campbell's real meaning behind *The Hero's Journey*.

Through its simple yet profound message, *Cassandra's Angel* ministers to the soul of the parent as well as the child. As your family shares this vision, you will see its effects on your children's sense of autonomy and self worth. This book is powerful medicine that you will want to read over and over again.

Stephen and Robin Larsen are authors of *A Fire in the Mind: The Life of Joseph Campbell*, and *The Fashioning of Angels: Partnership as Spiritual Practice*. Stephen is a psychotherapist in private practice who works with children as well as adults. Robin is a multi-faceted artist who runs programs for youth at risk. Together they direct the Center for Symbolic Studies in New Paltz, New York.

☆☆☆☆☆

DEDICATION

This book is lovingly dedicated to Marianne, my touchstone; Leo, my first friend on the path to the heart; Rosie, for not believing the story; and Manny, my promise fulfilled, my angel, my One.
Gina Otto

In memory of my beloved sister, Heidi.
Trudy Joost

☆☆☆☆☆

SPECIAL THANKS

Special thanks to Joni Albers, Robert A. Barton, Kari Brown, Avery Clayton, Madalena and Elena DeAndrea, Wayne Dyer, Melissa Etheridge, John Evans, Deborah Forman, Doug Freeman, Emily Freeman, Wade Freier, Dr. Michael Galitzer, Steve Hasenberg, Gerhard and Virginia Joost, Joyce La Conte, Robin and Stephen Larsen, C.S. Lewis, Megan Longenbaugh, Joanne Malisani, Paul Orfalea, Rob Parke, LouRay Partlow, Charley Randazzo, don Miguel Ruiz, Sharon Saks-Soboil, Lisa Shaw, Susan Smith-Jones, Michele Tamme, Murray Wecht, and Jo Ann Wood.

And very special thanks to John, Arrieana, and Ruth Thompson, Andrea Hurst, Cheryl Kerry, Bob Gruber, Cathy Sangster, Terri Cohlene and Trey Bornmann of Illumination Arts for their vision, love and support.

Cassandra's Angel

Written by Gina Otto ☆ Illustrated by Trudy Joost

ILLUMINATION Arts

PUBLISHING COMPANY, INC.

Cassandra, Cassandra was strolling along.
Cassandra was singing a sing-along song.
She ran through the house and into the hall.
She was just going to grab her red rubber ball...

When her mother's voice rang, as some mothers' do,
"Cassandra, come here. I must speak with you."

"Cassandra, Cassandra, your room is a mess.
Your toys are all over. There's jam on your dress.
Cassandra, whatever's the matter with you?
You've turned your whole bedroom into a zoo.

"I see lions and monkeys, some birds, and a bear.
There's no neatness to be found, not anywhere.
Cassandra, Cassandra, what am I to do?
You're a messy little girl. Just look at you."

Cassandra stopped to look around at the mess.
She looked at the zoo, then she looked at her dress.
Yes, indeed, it might all be true.
She just wasn't sure what she should do.

"I guess I'm a mess," was Cassandra's next thought,

"I guess I'm a mess," was Cassandra's next thought,
But she did not like that story — NO SHE DID NOT.

She picked up her toys and then changed her jam-dress.
She sang as she worked and cleaned up the whole mess.
Her entire zoo was put neatly away.
There would be no more messes in her room that day.

She took her red ball and went out to the yard.
That's where she saw Francine, and Ken, and Bernard.
"Do you want to play ball?" asked Cassandra with glee.
"Do you want to come over and play with me?"

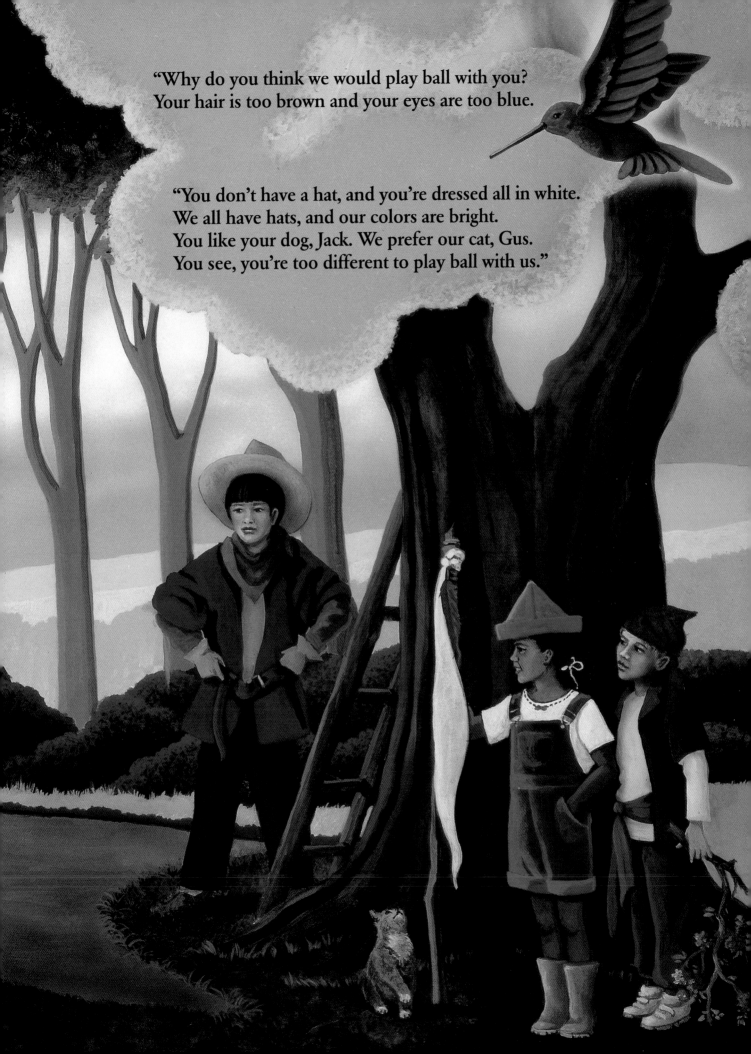

"Why do you think we would play ball with you?
Your hair is too brown and your eyes are too blue.

"You don't have a hat, and you're dressed all in white.
We all have hats, and our colors are bright.
You like your dog, Jack. We prefer our cat, Gus.
You see, you're too different to play ball with us."

Yes it was true, all the things those kids said.
They all had hats of blue, yellow, or red.
"My hair is different, and my eyes are too.
I'm feeling sad that my eyes are so blue.

"They don't like my clothes, and they don't like my dog.
So what would they think of my little pet frog?
I guess I'm too different," was Cassandra's next thought,

But she did not like that story — NO SHE DID NOT.

At school the next day, when it came time to paint,
"Class, here is your paper," said Mr. McQuaint.
"Your task is to paint a small house and a tree,
With seven red flowers and one yellow bee."

Cassandra didn't always remember each rule,
But she was determined to do well in school.
And boy, oh boy, did she love to paint.
How proud she was going to make Mr. McQuaint.

Cassandra took a big brush and let go a sigh.
She closed her eyes tightly and reached way up high.
She started to paint a magnificent tree.
It took all the room – none was left for the bee.

Then all of a sudden, her tree started growing,
Faster and faster, not stopping or slowing.
It spread from her easel to Mac's, then to Joe's,
And soon it took over the next seven rows.

With branches on Tom's pad, big leaves on Kate's,
This tree had oranges, pears, apples, and dates.
Her tree was so big it kept growing and soon
Its branches reached all the way up to the moon!

This tree was the grandest you ever could find,
And to think it all came from one little girl's mind.

Cassandra was painting a star at the top…

When a voice shrieked,
"Cassandra, you stop it now! STOP!"

Cassandra was looking around at the paint.
She looked at the room and at Mr. McQuaint.
"Cassandra, I'm giving your parents a call.
Now clean up this mess and go sit in the hall."

She picked up the branches and leaves in a flash,
And there was her tree stacked up high in the trash.

"I've done it again," she thought, out in the hall,
"But I really didn't mean to — no, not at all.

"The truth is I really don't know what I did.
I'm just doing my best at being a kid.
But no matter what, they just don't seem to see."
Then she sighed, "It was such a wonderful tree."

Soon Mr. McQuaint came out into the hall
With his face much more red than her red rubber ball.
"Cassandra, Cassandra, you're incorrigible, it's true.
What if all the children began acting like you?"

Cassandra was wondering what that big word meant.
It made her feel heavy, like a bag of cement.
If Mr. McQuaint said so, it must be true.
She just wasn't quite sure what she ought to do.

"I guess I'm incorrigible," was Cassandra's next thought,

But she did not like that story – NO SHE DID NOT.

On her way home she passed through Town Square,
And everyone acted like she was not there.
"There must be someone I can talk to or call."
Then she turned the corner and saw City Hall.

"I'll talk to the Mayor," she said with a grin,
So she marched up the stairs and then let herself in.

"The Mayor is busy," said Miss Iva Stress,
Whose big purple shoes matched her big purple dress.
"I'll wait," said Cassandra, "right here in this chair.
I'm hoping to talk with someone who will care."

Then out walked a very small man through the door,
With fists full of papers and shouting for more.
"Excuse me, Sir Mayor," she said, "if you're free,
I think it is you that I've come here to see.

"My mother says that my whole room is a zoo.
She just shakes her head, wondering what she should do.
I saw some children and asked them to play,
But they said mean things and then ran away.

"Today at my school, when I painted a tree,
I got paint on the classroom and all over me!
The tree that I made kept on growing and soon
It lifted our schoolhouse right up to the moon.

"So now they are all very angry with me.
I need someone's help, Mister Mayor, you see."

The Mayor stopped short on his way to the door
And dropped all his papers right there on the floor.
"What's all this nonsense about trees and a zoo?
I haven't got time to be talking with you.

"I have papers to sign, about seventy-four,
And when that's all done, I've got ninety-two more.
I have so much work, there is no time, I fear.
Now go home, little girl; you are not allowed here."

And before Cassandra could say any more,
Miss Iva Stress whisked her right out the door.
"He was my last hope," said Cassandra out loud.
But not one person heard in that very big crowd.

"I feel so alone," was Cassandra's next thought,

But she did not like that story — NO SHE DID NOT.

She started to run very fast — almost flying.
Cassandra hoped no one would see she was crying.
She soon found herself on the path by the lake.
"It just isn't fair, I am one big mistake.

"I am a mess. I'm a problem, you see.
I'm incorrigible, and they have no time for me.
Everyone believes it, which must make it true.
Even I start to believe it — well, I *almost* do.

"But deep down inside I know that I'm good,
Though most of the time I feel misunderstood.
I promise myself that I'll work through this test.
I'll try very hard and I'll do my best."

She climbed a big rock that was standing quite near
And then wiped away her very last tear.
She sat for a while on the rock all alone.
Then Cassandra stood, and she chose to go home.

"Somehow I will show them. Somehow they will see."
Then she turned and saw her magnificent tree.

And under her tree, sitting there on the ground…

Was a beautiful Angel, with wings and a crown.

"Who are you?" she asked, and again, "Who are you?"
The answer came softly, *Your Angel, that's who.*

I've been with you, Cassandra, since before you were born,
And it hurts me to see you so sad and forlorn.

So I've brought a great secret to give you today,
Come sit here beside me, Cassandra, please stay.

All of those things people have said to you,
They are stories, Cassandra — not one of them true.

You are never just what they believe you to be.
You are even more than you think that you see.

There's a much greater truth. When you look you will find
The key is right there in your heart and your mind.

It's not what you do — it's about who you are,
For you are as bright as the sky's brightest star.

All of the people who tell stories to you,
They each have the truth deep inside of them, too.

They have just forgotten it over the years,
So now what you hear is their sadness and fears.

It isn't their fault, all those stories they tell.
They believed the stories they were given as well.

Those old kinds of stories create guilt and fear,
But today, Cassandra, those old stories stop here.

You can love people more, for you know what is true.
You now have a choice. It is all up to you.

So shine brightly, Cassandra, to help light the way...
And that is the secret I bring you today.

With a soft breath of wind the Angel was gone,
And Cassandra could feel in her heart a new song...

"I'm Cassandra, a bright light," was her very next thought.
And no one could change *that* story – NO THEY COULD NOT!

P.O. Box 1865, Bellevue, WA 98009
Tel: 425-644-7185 ☆ 888-210-8216 (orders only) ☆ Fax: 425-644-9274
liteinfo@illumin.com ☆ www.illumin.com

☆☆☆☆☆

Library of Congress Cataloging-in-Publication Data

Otto, Gina, 1965-
    Cassandra's angel / written by Gina Otto ; Illustrated by Trudy Joost
        p.cm.
    Summary: When she listens to the people around her, Cassandra feels she cannot do
anything right, but then a meeting with her Angel gives her a new perspective on herself
and others.
    ISBN 0-935699-20-1 (hardcover)
    [1. Identity–Fiction. 2. Self-esteem–Fiction. 3. Interpersonal relations–Fiction. 4.
Angels–Fiction. 5. Stories in rhyme.] I. Joost, Trudy, 1949- ill. II. Title.

    PZ8.3.0845 Cas 2001
    [E]--dc21

                                                                    2001024536

☆☆☆☆☆

Published in the United States of America

Printed by Star Standard Industries in Singapore

Book Designer: Murrah & Company, Kirkland, WA

Art Production: Cheryl Kerry of Tahoma Organic, Tacoma, WA

ILLUMINATION ARTS PUBLISHING COMPANY, INC.
is a member of Publishers in Partnership – replanting our nation's forests.